City Council Boston, Mass.

Statue of Josiah Quincy

Dedication ceremonies, October 11, 1879. With preliminary proceedings

City Council Boston, Mass.

Statue of Josiah Quincy
Dedication ceremonies, October 11, 1879. With preliminary proceedings

ISBN/EAN: 9783337734343

Printed in Europe, USA, Canada, Australia, Japan

Cover: Foto ©Andreas Hilbeck / pixelio.de

More available books at **www.hansebooks.com**

JOSIAH QUINCY.

DEDICATION CEREMONIES,

OCTOBER 11, 1879.

With Preliminary Proceedings.

CITY DOCUMENT No. 115.

PRINTED BY ORDER OF THE CITY COUNCIL.
1879.

CITY OF BOSTON.

In Board of Aldermen, October 13, 1879.

Ordered, That the oration of His Honor the Mayor, delivered at the dedication of the Statue of Josiah Quincy, together with the presentation address of Alderman Tucker, and such other documents relating to the subject as may be of interest, be printed as a city document, under the direction of the Committee on Printing; and that five hundred extra copies be printed.

Read twice, and passed. Sent down for concurrence. October 23, came up, concurred. Approved by the Mayor October 25, 1879.

Attest :

S. F. McCLEARY,
City Clerk.

PRELIMINARY PROCEEDINGS.

At a meeting of the Board of Aldermen, July 12, 1875, the following communication was received from the Mayor : —

To the Board of Aldermen of the City of Boston : —

GENTLEMEN, — In 1861 the city received, under the will of Jonathan Phillips, the sum of $20,000, the income from which was to be expended in adorning and embellishing the streets and public places. In accepting the bequest, the City Council authorized the Board of Aldermen, with the approval of the Mayor, to expend the income in accordance with the terms of the trust. No expenditure has been made from the income up to this time, and the amount subject to the order of your Board on the first of May last was $18,160, a sum sufficiently large to make it proper for you to consider the manner in which the wishes of the testator shall be executed. Although the City Government can, under the terms of the will, spend the money annually for adornments of a temporary character, it would seem to be more in accordance with the spirit of the trust to invest it only in permanent works of art or beauty ; and this I conceive to have been the object of those who have preceded us allowing the fund to accumulate until it could be expended in a manner to do honor to the generosity of the founder. In calling your attention to the subject at this time, permit me to suggest that this money affords an opportunity for carrying out a proposition which has been frequently made, namely, to erect a statue in front of the City Hall, on the

right of the entrance from School street.   Among those who
have been mentioned as deserving subjects for such com-
memoration, Josiah Quincy stands foremost in the extent and
value of services rendered this municipality; and there would
be a special fitness in using this money for the purpose of
doing him honor.   ℮

SAMUEL C. COBB,

Mayor.

Referred, on motion of Alderman Prescott, to a special
committee, consisting of Aldermen Prescott, Pope, and
Viles.

At a meeting of the Board of Aldermen, October 18, 1875,
Alderman Prescott submitted the following report: —

The Special Committee of the Board of Aldermen, to whom
was referred the communication from His Honor the Mayor
in relation to the expenditure of the income from the bequest
of Jonathan Phillips, for adorning and embellishing the
streets and public places in this city, having carefully
considered the subject, beg leave to submit the following
report: —

It appears, from the language used in making the bequest,
that the purpose of the testator was to have the income expended annually; but as this has not been done, we are called
upon to consider the use to which it would be proper to apply
the fund which has been allowed to accumulate during the
past fourteen years, and which now amounts to something
over $18,000.

In his communication the Mayor suggests that it should be
used to procure a Statue of Josiah Quincy, the second Mayor
of this city, to be located in front of the City Hall.   The
committee have conferred with some of the leading citizens
of Boston, and find that the suggestion is generally received

with favor. If the money is to be used for the purpose of erecting a statue, there appears to be but one opinion as to the propriety of selecting Josiah Quincy, whose valuable services in organizing our municipal government will always be gratefully remembered by the citizens of Boston, and whose example, as an able, energetic, and upright magistrate, will ever continue to exert a powerful influence upon our municipal councils.

A question was raised by one of the gentlemen whom the committee consulted, and whose opinion is entitled to great weight, as to the propriety of using this money for the purpose of erecting any statue; but the City Solicitor decides that its use for such a purpose would not conflict with the terms of the trust. It does not appear that the testator had any very definite ideas as to the manner in which the income should be expended. He confided largely in the discretion of the City Government. An annual expenditure would, of course, preclude the erection of statues, on account of the smallness of the sum; but, in view of the fact that the income has been allowed to accumulate until it amounts to a considerable sum, there would seem to be no more appropriate way of perpetuating the generosity of the founder of the trust than by adopting the Mayor's suggestion.

The committee have made some inquiries in regard to the cost of a bronze statue, with a suitable pedestal, and find that the sum now subject to the order of Board is ample. They would, therefore, respectfully recommend the passage of the accompanying order : —

Ordered, That His Honor the Mayor, with three members of this Board, be a special committee with authority to contract for the delivery to this city of a bronze Statue of Josiah Quincy, second Mayor of Boston; and with authority also to contract for the construction of a suitable pedestal for said statue, to be located in front of the City Hall: the cost of the statue and pedestal not to exceed the sum of eighteen thousand dollars.

October 25th the order was amended by adding, "said sum to be paid from the income of the Phillips-street Fund, held by the Auditor of Accounts," and passed as amended.

Aldermen Charles J. Prescott, A. O. Bigelow, and Roland Worthington were appointed on the committee.

Soon after its appointment this committee met, and authorized its chairman to apply to William W. Story, of Rome, and Thomas Ball, of Florence, for models of a Statue of Quincy, offering five hundred dollars to the artist whose design should not be accepted.

At a meeting of the Board of Aldermen, January 10, 1876, Alderman Bigelow offered the following : —

"*Ordered*, That his Honor the Mayor, with Aldermen ——, be appointed to take charge of the erection of the proposed Statue of Josiah Quincy, with all the authority conferred by an order of the Board of Aldermen passed October 26, 1875."

Read twice and passed ; and Aldermen A. O. Bigelow, John T. Clark, and Thomas J. Whidden were appointed on the committee.

In 1876 models were received from the artists above named. Several gentlemen interested in art matters, together with the members of the Quincy family, were invited to inspect the models, and advise the committee as to their respective merits.

The verdict of the art critics was in favor of the model submitted by Mr. Story, while the Quincy family decided in favor of that made by Mr. Ball.

The committee decided to accept Mr. Ball's design, and a contract was therefore made with him to furnish a statue of heroic size, for the sum of twelve thousand dollars in gold.

In 1877 no committee was appointed, nor any further action taken.

At a meeting of the Board of Aldermen September 27, 1878, Alderman Whidden offered the following : —

"*Ordered*, That his Honor the Mayor, with Aldermen ——, be appointed to have charge of the erection of the Statue of Josiah Quincy, under the contract made with Thomas Ball."

Read twice and passed.; and Aldermen Thomas J. Whidden, John P. Spaulding, and Lewis C. Whiton were appointed on the committee.

In 1878 Mr. Ball was requested to furnish a design for a pedestal, which he did, and offered to superintend the construction of a pedestal of Italian marble, which he recommended as suitable for the purpose. This offer was accepted, and Mr. Ball was requested to construct a pedestal, according to his design, at a cost of eight hundred dollars.

At a meeting of the Board of Aldermen February 3, 1879, an order was passed similar in terms to the above order passed September 27, 1878, and Aldermen Joseph A. Tucker, Solomon B. Stebbins, and Daniel D. Kelly were appointed on the committee.

At a meeting of the Board of Aldermen, September 1, 1879, Alderman Tucker offered the following : —

"*Ordered*, That the Committee of the Board of Aldermen on the Erection of the Statue to Josiah Quincy, and the Joint Committee in charge of the Statue of Abraham Lincoln, acting together, be authorized to make suitable arrangements for the dedication of both of said structures on the 17th of September, 1879, — the expense attending the same, not exceeding five thousand dollars, to be charged to the appropriation for incidentals."

Read twice and passed.

September 15, 1879, on motion of Alderman Slade, the

2

Board of Aldermen reconsidered the above order; and, after discussion, on motion of Alderman Kelly, the subject was indefinitely postponed.

September 25, 1879, the Common Council passed the following : —

" *Ordered*, That the Committee of the Board of Aldermen on the Erection of the Statue of Josiah Quincy, and the Joint Special Committee in charge of the Statue Commemorating Emancipation, acting together, be authorized to make suitable arrangements for the dedication of both of said statues, — the expense attending the same, not exceeding one thousand dollars, to be charged to the appropriation for incidentals."

September 29 the order was passed in concurrence by the Board of Aldermen.

The Joint Special Committee in charge of the Statue Commemorating Emancipation was appointed as follows : —

June 3, 1879, Aldermen Charles H. B. Breck, Daniel D. Kelly, and Solomon B Stebbins :

June 5, 1879, Councilmen Henry W. Swift of Ward 9, Nathan Sawyer of Ward 18, Paul H. Kendricken of Ward 20, Oscar B. Mowry of Ward 11, and Benjamin F. Anthony of Ward 19.

October 9, 1879, on motion of Mr. Swift it was

" *Ordered*, That the use of the Common Council Chamber be allowed on Saturday next for the services of dedicating the Statue of Josiah Quincy, if the weather be unfavorable for conducting the services in the open air."

DESCRIPTION

QUINCY STATUE

The total height of the monument is eighteen feet seven inches. The base consists of a step and block of Quincy granite two feet nine inches high and seven feet eight inches square at the base. The pedestal and die, which are of Italian marble, give seven feet and ten inches more in height, and the die is four feet square. The die weighs seven tons, and the pedestal blocks about five tons each. The pedestal and die correspond in general design and size with those on which the figure of Franklin stands on the opposite side of the entrance to the City Hall, and a circular walk of concrete has been laid around the Statue, with a short walk connecting it with the paved approach to the hall entrance, this feature also corresponding with the surroundings of the Franklin statue. On the front of the die, facing School street, is a bronze plate, bearing the following inscription, in raised letters : —

JOSIAH QUINCY.
1772–1864.
MASSACHUSETTS SENATE, 1804.
CONGRESS, 1805–1813.
JUDGE OF MUNICIPAL COURT, 1822
MAYOR OF BOSTON, 1823–1828.
PRESIDENT OF HARVARD UNIVERSITY, 1829–1845.

On the side of the die facing the central walk is the following inscription, on a bronze plate : —

```
ERECTED A.D. 1879

FROM  FUNDS  BEQUEATHED

TO  THE  CITY  OF  BOSTON
                  BY
JONATHAN  PHILLIPS.
```

The other sides of the die are plain.

On the base block of the statue, facing the central walk, is inscribed, "Thomas Ball, Sc., 1878;" and on the reverse side of the block the founders' inscription, "Gegossen durch FERD. MILLER & Sohne, München, 1879."

The figure is, as will be seen, much above life size, and is thus made the more imposing. It is a noble work of art, and most creditable to the sculptor, Thomas Ball. The figure stands erect, with the weight posed on the right foot, the other foot being slightly advanced. Over the left shoulder is carelessly thrown a cloak, which appears to have slipped from the right shoulder, and the edge, passing beneath the right arm, is gathered up in front and held in the left hand, from which it hangs in heavy, bronze folds, while the right hand falls naturally by the side. This outer garment nearly conceals the lower part of the figure, and gives the opportunity for the classic disposition of drapery which most sculptors consider requisite to the best artistic effect. The disposition of the cloak is, however, such as to leave the outlines of the upper part of the figure clearly expressed beneath a coat closely buttoned, above which protrudes the old-fashioned, elaborated frill of the shirt front. The head is turned slightly to the right, and the pose as a whole is easy and most dignified and impressive. The countenance is said, by those best qualified to judge, to be an excellent likeness of the original. The light, brassy hue of the bronze, and its gloss, will be softened by time, — the bronze growing darker, and its gloss entirely disappearing. This change will favorably affect the lines of the figure, which will become less stiff and obtrusive, and the expression of the countenance will become more lifelike.

The work of erecting the monument was done under the direction of Mr. Clough, the City Architect, by ex-Alderman Thomas J. Whidden.

The cost of placing the Statue on the pedestal was defrayed by the artist. The cost of the pedestal, in Italy, was $800; its freight and insurance, $161.92. The front tablet cost $125, and the side tablet probably the same amount. The cost of foundation, filling, and grading around the same, providing two granite plinth blocks or sub-bases, and erecting the marble pedestal, was $933.48. $12,000 was paid for the Statue, making the aggregate of expenditure exceed $14,000, — defrayed by the Phillips Fund.

THE DEDICATION EXERCISES.

On Saturday, October 11, 1879, the dedicatory exercises were held in the Common Council Chamber, beginning at one o'clock. Arrangements had been made for the services about the Statue in the City Hall yard, but the uncertain state of the weather made it prudent to hold the exercises within doors. The Statue was unveiled by the City Architect, without ceremony, before several hundred people, gathered in School street and upon the City Hall green, at a few minutes before one o'clock.

Before the hour named for the exercises a large number of the invited guests assembled in the Mayor's office. The Quincy family was represented by ex-Mayor Josiah Quincy, Josiah P. Quincy, Esq., Gen. Samuel M. Quincy, Edmund Quincy, Esq., and Dr. Henry P. Quincy. There was also present Mr. William Hayden, who is nearly ninety years of age, and is the sole surviving representative of Mr. Quincy's administration, having served as Auditor.[1] The four vet-

---

[1] When, in the year 1823, Mr. Quincy entered upon his duties as Mayor of the City of Boston, his eager and searching investigation found, as among the principal reforms necessary to be made, the loose and irregular manner in which the money concerns had been conducted. In the second year of his administration, and as soon as more pressing affairs had been arranged, he set himself about to devise some fixed and regular mode of managing the financial affairs of the city. He wrote, with his own hand, the ordinance establishing the office of Auditor of Accounts, and instituting a system of finance which, through all the fluctuations of time and population, has amply answered its intended purposes ever since. Under the provisions of that ordinance Mr. William Hayden was elected the first Auditor of Accounts of the City of Boston, and continued to hold the office for nearly seventeen years. He returned the following answer to the invitation of the committee : —

erans of Quincy market — Messrs. Harmon Curtis, Nathan
Robbins, Jonathan Fletcher, and Ebenezer Holden, who
have been engaged in business there ever since the market
was erected — were also among the invited guests present,
as was Mr. Moses Williams, who was a member of the Common Council in 1822, and took an active interest in the prosperity of the market. The committees having had charge
of the erection of statues in former City Governments came
in response to invitations; and among the invited guests
who accepted were the Hon. Robert C. Winthrop, Hon.
Charles Francis Adams, ex-Mayor Samuel C. Cobb, ex-
Mayor Alexander H. Rice, Hon. Josiah G. Abbott, Gen.
N. P. Banks, Rev. Dr. Blagden, Gen. A. P. Martin, Rev.

"MALDEN, October 8, 1879.

HIS HONOR FREDERICK O. PRINCE, MAYOR OF THE CITY OF BOSTON: —

Dear Sir, — I have the honor to acknowledge receipt of an invitation of your committee of the City Council of Boston, to attend the ceremonies incident to the dedication of the Statue of Josiah Quincy, which invitation I thankfully accept, and shall
surely be present at the time assigned, if the weather and the infirmities of old age do
not interfere to prevent.

Of all the executive officers holding office under the City Council during the mayoralty of Mr. Quincy I am now the sole survivor, and it will be one among the many
reasons I have to be thankful to Divine Providence if I am permitted to participate
in the honors now to be paid to the memory of that illustrious citizen and magistrate.

I have treasured, as among the happiest incidents of my long life, my official connection with Mr. Quincy. The personal friendship which he was so kind as to bestow
upon me, and the constant and cordial good counsel and advice which I received from
him, have been of continuous and inestimable advantage to me. In those early days
he was 'my guide, philosopher, and friend.' I am happy to be allowed to bear this
testimony, being the only one of his subordinate municipal officers here on earth to
speak of him.

I will here repeat, with a feeling which the lapse of time has only increased, some
closing remarks made by me on another occasion, in regard to my connection with
Mr. Quincy: 'I was close to him — in daily contact with him — during nearly the
whole of his official career in the mayoralty. I was an admiring witness of his single-
hearted devotion, his unwearied assiduity, and his indomitable energy in the service
of the city. I honor and reverence the name and the memory of Josiah Quincy.'

With many thanks to your committee for the kindness of their invitation, I sub-
scribe myself, Mr. Mayor, respectfully,

Your friend and servant,

WILLIAM HAYDEN."

R. C. Waterston, George William Phillips, Rev. J. P. Bodfish, Mr. Thomas Ball, the sculptor, and past members of both branches of the City Government.

At a few minutes before one o'clock the invited guests, led by the Mayor and Honorable Josiah Quincy, proceeded to the Common Council Chamber.

At one o'clock the exercises began with a voluntary by the Germania Band.

Mayor Prince presented Rev. Dr. S. K. Lothrop, who offered the following

PRAYER.

Almighty God, our Heavenly Father, Thou art our God, and we will praise Thee; our fathers' God, and we will magnify Thy name. We thank Thee for this fair dwelling-place, which has come to us by inheritance. We recognize and adore that gracious providence which, through various trials and troubles, and the faithful efforts and sacrifices of successive generations, established our fathers in this land, and made them to dwell therein in safety, liberty, and independence. We recognize and adore that providence which has been rich in tokens of wisdom, goodness and mercy towards this city, from its earliest foundation until now, when it has become a city set on a hill, the light whereof cannot be hid, — a large, growing, prosperous, orderly Christian city, full of the institutions and influences of religion, education,

3

learning, art, science, philanthropy, commercial prosperity and enterprise, abounding in all things that
tend to adorn and elevate life. Lamenting the sins
that still prevail, we thank Thee for the general intelligence and honorable character which have com-
monly marked our people, and especially we praise
Thee for all the good, noble and distinguished men,
whom from time to time Thou hast raised up to be
guides and leaders of public thought and action, and
whose example and instructions in every department
of life made them a blessing and a benefit to their
generations, so that their names come down to us in
honored remembrance.

We thank Thee especially for the life, character,
and services of him to whose honor and memory we
here and now gratefully erect this Statue. O God!
let Thy blessing rest upon this work of our hands and
expression of our hearts. Let this Statue abide for
long years and successive generations, and while it
presents to us who remember him, and will ever present to those who come after us, a clear and striking
delineation of his form and person, may it ever and
always speak to us, and to the successive generations
as they pass, of his worth, and virtues, and usefulness;
of his industry in improving every talent entrusted,
every opportunity offered to him; of his integrity ever
unimpeached, his honor unstained, his fidelity to

every trust; of the simplicity, purity, patriotism and piety that marked, pervaded and imbued his character and conduct in all the scenes and largely varied offices and responsibilities which he was called to assume in his long and useful life; and thus, O God, grant that his memory may abide, and enshrined here on this spot, may it be an incentive to all to imitate him in all social, civil, patriotic and Christian duty.

Let Thy blessing, O God, rest upon the present Chief Magistrate of our city, and upon all associated with him in the management of our municipal affairs, that they may be faithful to their trusts, and promote in all directions the best interests of our people. Let Thy blessing rest upon everything dear and valuable to this community and to our country. Stay the strife of parties and pour oil upon the troubled waters everywhere. Here among ourselves, and everywhere throughout our broad land, in all sections of it, let there prevail more and more a spirit that shall bind us all together, as one people, in the holy fellowship of patriotic duty, and of pure and holy living — that righteousness which alone exalteth — which we ask to the glory of Thy holy name in Christ Jesus, our Lord, ascribing unto Thee everlasting praises. Amen.

Alderman Tucker, chairman of the Statue Committee, then presented the Statue to the Mayor, as follows :—

ALDERMAN TUCKER'S ADDRESS.

Mr. Mayor, — It becomes my pleasant duty, as a representative of the legislative department of the City Council, to surrender to you this Statue of Josiah Quincy, who, in the early history of this city, made an illustrious record in the position you now hold as Mayor of Boston. This duty is rendered especially gratifying from the fact that this Statue represents the first fruits of the beneficent spirit which actuated our fellow-citizen, Jonathan Phillips, when he donated the fund from which its cost is defrayed. Mr. Phillips died in 1860, leaving a legacy of $20,000 to the City of Boston, providing that the income thereof should be expended by the Board of Aldermen, with the approval of the Mayor, to adorn and embellish the streets and public places of the city; and, for the first time since the bequest was made, we are assembled together to witness material evidence of the testator's generosity. It is, sir, both fortunate and appropriate, that the subject chosen should be one whose foresight and wisdom rendered him conspicuous in the history of the municipality, and who dictated a line of policy which, being pursued by his successors, has not only done much to embellish our city, but has also been fruitful in more substantial advantages. It is not fitting at this time that I should pronounce any encomiums on Josiah Quincy. Upon you, Mr. Mayor, not more from the position you now hold, than by early and intimate relations with Mr. Quincy during his life, devolves this honorable privilege. But allow me to say that I believe it will afford the greatest satisfaction to our citizens to see this tribute to the memory of one who did so much for the city he governed so well.

Mayor Prince received the Statue in behalf of the city, and pronounced the following Oration, at the conclusion of which the benediction was pronounced by Dr. Lothrop, and the audience dispersed to music by the Band.

ORATION,

FREDERICK O. PRINCE,

MAYOR.

Gentlemen of the City Council and Fellow-Citizens : —

The Honorable Jonathan Phillips, who died in 1860, gave by his will to the City of Boston, "the sum of twenty thousand dollars as a trust fund, the income from which shall be annually expended to adorn and embellish the streets and public places in said city." In accepting the bequest, the City Council directed the Board of Aldermen, with the approval of the Mayor, to expend the income of the fund in compliance with the terms of the trust.

This donation was received in 1861, but nothing was done in fulfilment of the objects of the testator until the year 1875, when my predecessor, Mayor Cobb, finding the income of the fund had accumulated so largely as to demand and justify some action in the direction of the trust, advised the erection of a statue in front of City Hall and opposite to that of

Franklin. He took the occasion to suggest the fitness of commemorating by such a monument the municipal and other public services of Josiah Quincy. The special committee of the Board of Aldermen, to whom was referred the recommendation of His Honor, reported that "if the money is to be used for the purpose of erecting a statue, there appears to be but one opinion as to the propriety of selecting that of Josiah Quincy, whose valuable services in organizing our municipal government will always be gratefully remembered by the citizens of Boston, and whose example, as an able, energetic, and upright magistrate will ever continue to exert a powerful influence upon our municipal councils." Accompanying the report was an order authorizing the erection of a statue of this distinguished man.

I need not say that the action of the Government in this matter expressed the sentiments and received the hearty approval of our citizens.

Soon after the passage of the order a contract was made for the work with that eminent Boston artist, Thomas Ball.

It now stands before you. There may be differences of opinion, resulting from differences in æsthetic tastes and judgment, touching the artistic merits of this statue. We rarely find in art-criticism entire concordance; but I think it will be generally regarded

as a faithful, successful, and elegant representation of
him we honor to-day. If I am right in this we have
fulfilled the testamentary desires of our munificent
benefactor, for the image of one so much respected
and beloved will assuredly " adorn and embellish "
this " public place of the city."

Mr. Quincy was so well known to the citizens of
Boston, he was before them so many years of his
long and useful life, and filled so many important
offices, that it seems unnecessary and superfluous for
me, even were I fitted for the grateful task, to portray
at length his character, or recite his many public services. It has already been done, and well done, by
the hand of filial affection. I can say nothing new
of the subject. But it is expected that on this occasion I should glance upon some of the prominent
features of Mr. Quincy's character, and refer to some
of the important acts of his life, not only for the
information of the younger portion of our citizens,
who came upon the stage of life after his official career had ended, and therefore had not the same op-
portunities of knowing him as those who were about
him; but for the benefit of those to be found in every
community — strange as it may seem — who, living
near the age of distinguished men, have often little
or no knowledge of their lives or actions. The accomplished biographer of Mr. Quincy tells us in the

4

preface to his most delightful book that he had met
" well-educated persons who had never heard of
Fisher Ames, and even gentlemen of the law whose
notions of Samuel Dexter were nebulous to the last
degree."

Mr. Quincy inherited a name distinguished in
several generations for the highest civic virtues, for
patriotism, public spirit, love of liberty, respect for
law, hatred of wrong, sympathy for suffering, and
sacred regard for honor. His father — known in
history as Josiah Quincy, Junior — was one of the
organizers and brilliant orators of the Revolution.
He was eminent, notwithstanding his early death at
the age of thirty-three, among the great men who
moulded public opinion and guided public action in
those eventful days. Many of his great qualities
were transmitted to his son. The youth of the
latter was carefully trained by a wise and devoted
mother, and he early felt the desire and recognized
the duty of moral and mental cultivation " as the
noblest of human pursuits." He showed his deep
sense of the importance of this cultivation by upbraid-
ing himself on one occasion, notwithstanding his
great and conscientious industry in his studies, for
not having done more, and resolving " to be more
circumspect in future; to hoard his moments with
more thrifty spirit; to listen less to the suggestions of

indolence, and so quicken that spirit of intellectual improvement to which he devotes his life."

The inscription upon the pedestal of the statue informs the spectator that Josiah Quincy was born in 1772 and died in 1864; that he served the people as State Senator, as representative to the National Congress, as one of the judges, as Mayor of Boston, and as President of Harvard University. The record shows that in all these important capacities he acted well his part, and made the people his debtors.

He seems to have had a Spartan conviction that his time, his talents, and all his services were due to the State; for, during his long life, — extended beyond his ninety-second birthday, — it may be said that he was constantly employed, either in official service or in illustrating by his pen political subjects, or subjects in which the public was interested. He did not allow himself rest even after he had attained the great age of eighty years, for he then commenced the composition of his admirable life of that distinguished statesman and philosopher, John Quincy Adams. I may add in respect to his writings that he touched nothing which he did not adorn with a wealth of solid information and valuable and instructive reflection. It is remarkable that he retained his mental powers for so many years without showing evidence of decay or decrepitude. This is without doubt due to his tem-

perance, his industry, his systematic habits, and his
great love of work.

In 1793 Mr. Quincy was admitted to the bar. He
was then twenty-one years of age. The practice of
the law does not seem to have been congenial to his
tastes, for he did not continue long in it. In 1798 he
was selected to deliver the Fourth-of-July oration at
the town celebration of the anniversary of independence, and the reputation he obtained by it induced
the Federalists to select him as their candidate
for representative to Congress. He was then only
twenty-eight years old, and his biographer observes
that his age was considered so infantile that the
Democratic papers called aloud for a cradle in which
to rock the Federal candidate. He was not successful at this election, although he had a majority of the
votes of the town of Boston, then only a part of the
first congressional district.

In the spring of 1804 he was elected to the State
Senate, and in November of the same year, having
been again nominated by the Federalists as their candidate, he was chosen representative to the Ninth
Congress.

Mr. Quincy at once made the most diligent and
thorough preparation for the discharge of his congressional duties, his studies embracing history and
politics, especially that part of both subsequent to

the adoption of the federal constitution. Party spirit at this period was most intense and bitter. The Federalists were greatly in the minority in both branches of Congress; but they comprised many of the ablest and most eminent men of the country. Mr. Quincy took at once a prominent position among them, which he held during all the eight years he served in Congress.

As we look at his public character, he appears to us as a successful *orator*, an accomplished *statesman*, and an able *magistrate*.

Let us consider him in these relations. His culture, his classic learning, his stores of historical and political information, his earnest interest in whatever engaged his attention, his zeal and enthusiasm, his manly form, full of grace, dignity, and power, must have made his oratory most impressive and effective. His forensic efforts did not, indeed, exhibit that rare and lofty eloquence which distinguished those great orators of ancient and modern times, who still stir the blood, after the occasion, the scene, and the cause have passed away; but his advocacy was so forcible, and marked by such strength of reason and felicity of illustration, as to call forth not only the admiration of those who thought as he did concerning public affairs, but of his political opponents.

All the testimony shows that at times — indeed generally — his manner was earnest and impassioned to the highest degree. His language, when now read, shows it must have been so. His rhetoric was most fervid and glowing. He had a ready and sparkling wit, a delicate and pleasing humor, and such capacity for sarcasm and invective as must have made him formidable when excited in debate. Yet he seems at all times, even in the "tempest and whirlwind of passion," to have "a temperance," so as neither to impair the force of his argument nor give advantage to his opponent. He had the courage of his convictions most forcibly. He followed a principle wherever it led, whatever the consequences to his cause or himself; and always, perhaps unwisely at times, said what he thought.

He often pressed the fight so sharply that apprehension was sometimes felt by his friends for his personal safety; but fear was not a part of his nature, and he always scorned the notion of danger, and rejected all advice to arm himself against attack. It was evident that whatever differences of opinion existed between Mr. Quincy and his political opponents, and however greatly they have been irritated against him at times for language in debate, they respected his manly nature, the purity of his motives,

the honesty of his opinions, and his conscientious
discharge of duty according to his convictions.

He spoke on all the important questions which
came before Congress, and always with the same
earnestness and zeal. He could hardly do otherwise,
for he felt intensely in respect to everything which,
in his judgment, affected the interests, the safety, or
the honor of the country. He was so organized that
to follow his convictions was a necessity. Morally as
well as physically brave, to an extraordinary degree,
he would not, because he *could* not, compromise a
principle. He was

"Too fond of the right to pursue the expedient."

He felt, like Milton's angel, that

"To be weak was miserable."

Once, therefore, satisfied as to the course which duty
required him to follow, he followed it, wholly un-
mindful of personal costs or consequences.

I cannot forbear quoting his own words in this
connection: "I mean to identify myself with no set
of men. I shall do my duty openly, virtuously, and
as intelligently as Heaven permits me. I shall not
seek to please by any sacrifice of my real opinions.
I shall not fear to offend any, if a just view of my
country's interest obliges me to declare truths which

will have that effect.   This course of conduct will not secure me place,— of which I am less than ever solicitous,— but it will secure me that sense of right to personal honor, of which I am daily more and more solicitous."

His distinguished father, when reproached for defending the British soldiers indicted for the Boston massacre, declared that he "never harbored the expectation, nor any great desire, that all men should speak well of him.   To inquire my duty and to do it is my aim."

Can any one doubt that the same blood flowed in the veins and animated the hearts of these two men?

Mr. Quincy, in his early political life, clearly saw the dangers to the Republic from the institution of slavery; and unrestrained by considerations of personal interest or advantage, and impelled alone by conscientious regard for duty, took every occasion to express his opinions in relation to it.   Earnestly and with all his power he protested against every measure which seemed to him directed to its extension beyond its limits at the adoption of the Federal Constitution. These protests are marked by great vigor of language, and will be found to contain some of the best specimens of impassioned eloquence which American oratory can boast.   Mr. Webster has said that the

speeches of Mr. Quincy in Congress were the best
and ablest ever delivered in that body on the influence of slavery.

It cannot be denied that Mr. Quincy possessed in
an eminent degree the qualities of a *statesman*.

From his first entrance into political life he com-
prehended fully the many important questions which
then occupied public attention, and understood clearly
what the true interests of the country demanded. He
saw with prophetic accuracy the future results of the
foreign and domestic policy of the party in power,
detected with equal clearness the troubles to come
from that box of Pandora, — the slavery question, —
and predicted the consequences which would follow
any attempts to extend the institution into new
Territories and States.

We may dissent from many of his political views,
and doubt the wisdom of many of the measures he
advocated touching these great questions, without
detracting from his claims to sagacity or discounting
his title to statesmanship. It is to be remembered
that the genius, spirit, and powers of the Federal
Constitution were not then as well understood as
now. The relations of the Federal Government and
the States to each other, their mutual rights and
obligations (not yet fully recognized and adjusted,

but then less known than now), were the subjects of constant sectional discussion and controversy.

The wild and radical speculations of the French Revolutionists touching government as a science, the rights of man, the social compact, and other questions of metaphysical politics, had intoxicated the country with their delirious fumes, largely affected the sentiments and opinions of the people, and created party divisions of the most intense and hostile character.

It is not strange that under these circumstances statesmanship should have been tainted with partisanship, and that the public men on both sides should have often viewed political measures from mere party stand-points, and not in that broad and catholic spirit which patriotism required and the interests of the country demanded.

The study of Mr. Quincy's speeches in Congress, and the examination of his votes, show that he was a most intense Federalist, firm in the faith that his party was always right and monopolized the largest share of the patriotism of the times. Notwithstanding, however, the fixedness of his political opinions, he was always open to the influence of reason, although, as with most men of strong convictions, it might be sometimes difficult to make him feel its force and recognize an error of judgment. But he did not belong to that unyielding class, now so common, I regret to say, who exult that they are so organized as not to be open to conviction. There were occasions when Mr. Quincy saw that the ties of party should not bind him, and they were ignored. A notable instance of this occurred when he voted for the bill to increase the navy at the time war with England was imminent, notwithstanding the Federalists opposed the measure, and he knew he should incur the censure of his party for his independent action.

In subsequent years, when Mr. Quincy acted with the Whigs, he ignored all party ties whatever, and allowed no party dictation to control his actions touching measures which, in his judgment, were repugnant to the honor and interests of the country.

Statesmanship is but common sense and common honesty applied to public affairs, but the greatest of these is honesty. On these two essentials hang all the law and gospel of statesmanship. He who recognizes the duties of government to the people, and the obligations and duties of nations to each other according to the dictates of justice and fair dealing, and has the courage to do what he knows to be right, is a *statesman*.

He may not have the statecraft of a Machiavelli or a Richelieu or a Talleyrand or a Bismarck, but he will be better fitted to guide the ship of state, and accomplish the great ends of government, — the prosperity and happiness of the people.

The principles which guided Mr. Quincy's political action and illustrated his statesmanship are well expressed in his oration at the celebration of the completion of the second century from the settlement of Boston. "What," says he, "are the elements of the liberty, prosperity, and safety, which the inhabitants of New England at this day enjoy? Those elements are simple, obvious, and familiar. Every civil and religious blessing of New England, all that has given happiness to human life or security to human virtue, is alone to be perpetuated in the forms and under the auspices of a free Commonwealth. The Commonwealth itself has no other strength or hope than the intelligence and virtue of individuals who compose it. For the intelligence and virtue of individuals there is no other human assurance than laws providing for the education of the whole people. These laws themselves have no strength or efficient sanction except in the moral and accountable nature of man disclosed in the records of the Christian faith. The great comprehensive truths, written in letters of living light on every page of our history, the language addressed by every past age of New England to all future ages, is this: 'Human happi-

ness has no perfect security but freedom; freedom
none but virtue; virtue none but knowledge; and
neither freedom, nor virtue nor knowledge has any
vigor or immortal hope except in the principles of
the Christian faith, and in the sanctions of the
Christian religion.'"

Such sentiments are conclusive proof that he
who uttered them was not only a statesman, but
a Christian.

As a magistrate and an executive officer Mr.
Quincy's capacity was most conspicuous.

When Boston first became a city, although opposed
to the acceptance of a city charter, in the belief that
the town organization was better suited to the character and genius of the New England people than
the less democratic government of a civic corporation,
the prominent citizens felt that he was best fitted to
organize and administer the new form of government. He had already greatly interested himself in
many matters of municipal concern, especially in
those relating to the provision for the poor and the
treatment of the vicious and criminal. In 1821, as
chairman of a legislative committee charged with
the consideration of these subjects, he had submitted
a most exhaustive and instructive report thereon;
and was soon afterward appointed chairman of a

town committee on the same matter. Upon his recommendation provision had been made for a House of Industry, and a suitable building erected at South Boston on a tract of land bought for the purpose. As judge of the Municipal Court he had in his charges to the grand jury considered the treatment of criminals, and indicated the reforms which the civilization of the age and the welfare of society demanded.

I may here observe that Mr. Quincy presided on the 28th of March, 1822, as the moderator of the last town meeting ever held by the inhabitants of Boston in Faneuil Hall.

The nomination for mayor was tendered him by a large body of the citizens, irrespective of party; but both Federalists and Democrats saw fit to nominate candidates, and he wanted about one hundred votes for a majority. On a second trial he withdrew his name, and Mr. John Phillips was elected the first mayor of Boston. Upon the retirement of the latter, at the close of the year, Mr. Quincy was elected, almost without opposition, his successor.

He was eminently fitted for the place; for he brought to the discharge of its duties great powers of organization, great capacity for work, great industry, remarkable directness and celerity of action, and excellent judgment. His love of labor and

desire for improvement kept him constantly busy,
and every municipal department felt his influence.

Immediately upon entering upon the duties of his
office he made himself chairman of all the aldermanic
committees, and personally supervised and directed
the various matters under their charge, doing generally the largest part of the work. He introduced
many salutary changes and important reforms, by
which he promoted the comfort, increased the safety,
and improved the beauty of the city. Without
attempting any detailed account of his official work,
I will merely say that under his administration pau-
pers and criminals were separated and cared for; the
House of Correction and the House of Reformation
for juvenile offenders established; the police and fire
departments reorganized; various improvements introduced into the public-school system, and the
Faneuil Hall market-house erected.

It seems to me proper to say here a few words
touching the services of Mr. Quincy in respect to
the establishment of this last-named most important
civic institution.

Without imposing the tax or the debt of a dollar
upon the city, he filled the old Town Dock, so called;
removed large numbers of old and worthless build-
ings occupied by the lowest of the population, and
constituting the Five Points of Boston; laid out

anew the territory so as to make six new streets, besides greatly enlarging another; constructed extensive docks and built a granite market-house, two stories high, five hundred and thirty-five feet long and fifty feet wide, covering twenty-seven thousand square feet of land. The lots made by filling the dock, and the improved value of the estates bought by the city to carry out the enterprise more than paid for its cost. Few can appreciate the extent and importance of this improvement who do not know the character and appearance of this part of the city before it was made.

The scheme when first suggested was, of course, opposed, as all great public improvements usually are. The timid doubt success; the cautious fear expense; the conservative oppose change; the demagogue springs the rattle of misrepresentation and detraction, so that the people are embarrassed to discriminate between a wise and an unwise economy. Our city has had and is having many such experiences.

The zeal and good management of Mr. Quincy surmounted every obstacle and overcame all opposition. To him, and him alone, belongs the credit of this great work. It may be said, and truly said, that if he had distinguished his administration by nothing else, this important structure, and the improvement of the territory in its vicinity, would have alone made his name honorable to the citizens and justified the erection of this statue to his memory. But no monument is needed to perpetuate the remembrance of his services in this work. The work itself is his monument. We can point to it and say of him, as was said of the architect of St. Paul's: —

" *Si monumentum requiris, circumspice.*"

But it was not merely because he improved the architecture of Boston, nor because he organized and established penal, reformatory, and eleemosynary institutions, that Mr. Quincy is honored by a grateful city. He was most energetic in the enforcement of the laws, in the correction of abuses, in the protection of the rights of the city, and in the introduction of systematic and economic methods in the transaction of municipal business. He loved Boston. He was proud of its history, of its Revolutionary record, of its devotion to the great principles of civil and religious liberty, and of the influence of its citizens in shaping the institutions of the country. He loved it "as an Athenian loved the city of the violet crown; as a Roman loved the *Maxima rerum Roma.*" "In Boston," says he, "I was born. In Boston I have lived, and from Boston I choose to be buried."

It is right that Boston should honor him. It is

not too much to say that our city is to-day in a better
condition — its public institutions better, its name
and reputation better, and its honor higher — because
Josiah Quincy was mayor for six years.

There were some improvements suggested by him
which we all now regret were not made; if they had
been, the city would to-day be enjoying greater comfort, convenience, health, and beauty. Mr. Quincy,
in his policy, did not confine himself merely to the
necessities of the present. He believed that Boston
was destined to be a metropolis, and he wished to
provide for the wants of such. There is no doubt
that if some of his designs had been carried out we
should have saved many of the millions we have
been compelled to spend in widening streets and in
other civic accommodations. We can yet entitle
ourselves to the gratitude of the future by taking
counsel of his wise foresight and his expanded views
of municipal requirements.

Public benefactors not unfrequently fail of appre-
ciation in their lifetime. The reforms and improvements made by Mr. Quincy in the interest of good
government aroused the opposition of some who
were disturbed by them. This was to be expected.

" No man e'er felt the halter draw,
    With good opinion of the law."

As he said in his first inaugural, " In administering the police, in executing the laws, in protecting the rights and promoting the prosperity of the city, its first officer will be necessarily beset and assailed by individual interests, by rival projects, by personal influences, by party passions. The more firm and inflexible he is in maintaining the rights and pursuing the interests of the city, the greater the probability of his becoming obnoxious to the censure of all whom he causes to be prosecuted or punished, of all whose passion he thwarts, of all whose interests he opposes." "No man," says he, on another occasion, "could do his duty in this office without being turned out of it."

Mr. Quincy's prophecy proved true in his own case. He had been reëlected five times. Misrepresentation and detraction organized a strong opposition against him. At the next election he failed to receive a majority of the votes and withdrew from the contest, when Mr. Otis was elected to his place.

No one to-day believes in the charges made against him by his opponents. No one doubts his administrative ability, his sagacious judgment in the management of civic affairs, his untainted honesty, and his spotless integrity. The charges and accusations of his enemies have dissipated through their utter groundlessness. I once saw somewhere a picture representing some foolish archers shooting their harmless arrows at the sun. Beneath the picture was written *Solem nulla sagitta ferit:* No arrow strikes the sun. It well illustrates the impotency of political slander. The arrows aimed at Mr. Quincy fell far short of their mark, and made no wound.

Nothing shows more the manliness of Mr. Quincy's nature than his valedictory declaration, "that he retired from office with a consciousness weighed against which all human suffrages were but as the light dust of the balance." He seems, however, to have felt a moment's pain, as we can easily believe, that after so much time and labor expended in behalf of the citizens; after having accomplished so much for the lasting benefit of the city and for the promotion of its interests; after all his faithful, honest, and disinterested service, — he should have been thus requited. But doubtless he consoled himself with the philosophic reflection that other officials before him had been as badly treated, and others after him would share the same fate; that, if he was patient, time, which at last makes all things even, would permit party prejudice to subside, so that the record could be made up according to justice and truth.

Upon the retirement of Mr. Quincy from the mayoralty, the friends and Fellows of Harvard College saw that his great administrative abilities eminently fitted him for the presidency of that insti-

tution, which was then vacant. Its financial affairs
were at that time greatly confused, and a practical
man of business was needed to put them in proper
condition.

He was unanimously nominated by the corporation
for the office, and the nomination was subsequently
confirmed by the Board of Overseers. He held the
place for sixteen years, and it is generally admitted
that his administration was a great success.

This occasion does not permit me to point out the
particular reforms he accomplished, nor the various
improvements he introduced into that institution. To
do so would require more time than would be proper
for me to ask, or you to give. I will only say that
they were many and important, and have resulted in
lasting benefit to the college.

President Walker, — Mr. Quincy's third successor,
— whose official position gave him ample knowledge
of what the latter had accomplished, says: "I have
been led to review with some care his administration
of the college, and the effect of it has been greatly to
increase my sense of the obligation the college is
under to him. Sixteen years of more devoted, unre-
mitting, unwearied work in the service of a public
institution were never spent by mortal man; and
when we call to mind the state of things at the
time of the appointment, it seems to me that he will

be forever remembered as the great organizer of the university."

Such was Josiah Quincy as orator, statesman, and magistrate. He was more than these; he was a true patriot and a Christian gentleman. To say this of any one is to say all that eulogy requires.

The patriotism of Mr. Quincy was of the purest and most exalted character. During all his long and well-spent life his heart was full of care and solicitude for his country. He was ever concerned for the reputation, the honor, and the interests of the republic and its institutions. Whatever affected the cause of liberty, civil and religious, affected him. He would have made any sacrifices demanded by patriotism, whatever the personal cost or consequence. If he had lived in the days which tried men's souls, he would have uttered the same revolutionary eloquence which distinguished his illustrious sire, and perhaps been found on the same battle-field where fell his father's friend, the immortal Warren. His heroic nature is well shown in his benedictive letter to his grandson on his departure for the war then waging for the preservation of the Union. I know nothing in modern language so touching and pathetic. It glows with all the patriotic spirit of the Spartan mother arming her son for the battle, refined by those humane sentiments which the cruel policy of that martial race so severely repressed, and sanctified by the tenderness natural to consanguinity. His ardent love of country, his recognition of the duties of the citizen in the great crisis, his pride in the patriotism of the young soldier who shared his blood and bore his honored name, and his tender affection for him, are all most feelingly and eloquently expressed. No one can doubt where Josiah Quincy would have been in the recent contest of the country for its life but for the impeding weight of his great age.

His patriotism led him to a firm belief in the ultimate success of the Union cause. He never doubted from the first that the integrity of the government would be maintained. This assurance was not born of *hope*, the sentiment of the weak; it was the child of *faith*, which is the conviction of the strong. He could not believe, he would not believe, that this great country, with its free government, the best adapted for the promotion of human happiness which ingenuity has ever devised, or the world ever seen, the hope of the oppressed of all nations, could be broken up and destroyed. He died before the flag of secession went down: but he closed his eyes as well assured of what the end would be as though he

heard the shouts of our victorious columns on the
surrender at Appomattox Court-House.

We owe to Mr. Quincy infinite gratitude for the
instructive example he has given the world of the
usefulness of *old age*, and of the unwisdom of growing old. Most men think that when "the way of life
is fallen into the sere, the yellow leaf," the season
and duty of work is over, that they must then hiber-
nate like the irrational animals. Not so thought Mr.
Quincy. He kept his intellectual faculties bright
by their constant use, and retained to the last his
interest in all the matters and things which had occupied his attention through life, especially in those
which concerned the country. He felt it a duty not
to grow old before it was necessary, and that time in
his judgment never comes until the capacity for
useful action is gone. He was ever engaged in some
intellectual occupation, and as fast as one work was
completed, another was undertaken. He recognized
the obligation to men in the Hebrew poem —

"They shall bring forth fruit in old age."

"There is no period of a man's life," says a witty
and distinguished divine, " in which he has a right to
put himself on the shelf ; there are but two persons
who have the right to lay you aside, — your doctor

and the sexton. Every man owes to himself and to his kind, as an example that is influential upon the young, the continued exertion of his ripe powers to the very end of life." So thought Mr. Quincy, and so thinking he acted; and so should all men think and act when they remember what capacity for thought and action has been implanted within them by the Divine Creator, and the sin of permitting this capacity to

— "rust in us unused."

The City of Boston has erected statues to commemorate those who have had more genius, a broader intellect, a larger culture; and who attained a loftier niche in the temple of fame than he whom we honor to-day? Here at our side is the monument of Franklin; not far off stand those of Everett, Webster, and, the greatest of this triumvirate, Hamilton; the magnificent statue of the peerless Washington is the admiration of all who enter the Public Garden; but I venture the assertion that none of these has made a more faithful use of such talents as God gave him, recognized more conscientiously the obligations of duty, or left a more spotless name. His honor is without stain. His record will be vainly searched for any coarse, vulgar, or dishonest act. His life exhibits the simple virtues, the plain, upright bearing and conduct of one who feared God, and God only: of

one who possessed that most valuable of all posses-
sions,— *self-respect.*

At the great age of ninety-two years, surrounded
by all

> — " which should accompany old age,
> As honor, love, obedience — troops of friends."

he died.

The city has wisely erected this monument to commemorate her benefactor. The spot is well chosen.
It not only stands in a "public place," in accordance
with the testamentary direction of Mr. Phillips, but
beside the statue of Franklin, the friend of both the
father and grandfather of our distinguished mayor.
If we could believe that bronze might feel and speak,
what welcome would the great philosopher, patriot,
and statesman, give his companion as he mounts his
pedestal! With what interest would the two review
the eventful past, and how would they exult and con-
gratulate each other that our terrible civil war was at
last ended; the States no longer " dissevered, discord-
ant, belligerent;" the flag everywhere respected, and
the country commencing a new career of prosperity
and glory! "

May this image of our great and good magistrate
not only adorn and embellish Boston, but inspire
those who shall be called to execute the civic trusts

he administered so well, to imitate his official probity, fidelity, and zeal, that the prosperity of our beloved city may be advanced, and its honor maintained in the coming centuries.

www.ingramcontent.com/pod-product-compliance
Lightning Source LLC
Chambersburg PA
CBHW022202020726
47496CB00008B/2833

*9 7 8 3 3 3 7 7 3 4 3 4 3 *